Shimmer
the Magic Ice Pony

For Laura x – SK

To Tom & Drew xx – ST

SIMON AND SCHUSTER

First published in Great Britain in 2011 by Simon and Schuster UK Ltd

1st Floor, 222 Gray's Inn Road, London WC1X 8HB

A CBS Company

A CIP catalogue record for this book is available from the British Library upon request

ISBN: 978 0 85707 107 1

Printed in China

1 3 5 7 9 10 8 6 4 2

Princess Evie's Ponies

Shimmer the Magic Ice Pony

Sarah KilBride
Illustrated by Sophie Tilley

SIMON AND SCHUSTER
London New York Sydney

It was such a cold day at Starlight Stables that even the water buckets had frozen! Princess Evie gave each of her ponies fresh water and straw.

“Now, who would like to warm up with an adventure?” she said. You see, Princess Evie’s ponies were magic ponies. Whenever Evie rode them, she was whisked away on a magical adventure in a faraway land.

"Shimmer!" said Evie. "Would you like to come?"
Shimmer tossed her long silver mane. She loved adventures!

When Sparkles the kitten heard Evie getting her rucksack of useful things, he raced across the yard to join them.

Off they cantered, through the
frosty fields to the tunnel of trees.
Evie closed her eyes. Where would the
tunnel take them today?

Shimmer's hooves echoed as they walked out of a huge ice cave.

Princess Evie was lovely and snug in the snow boots and furry coat that she now wore. Ice crystals glinted in Shimmer's mane and tail, and rows of tiny icicles twinkled from her reins. Outside the cave, sat a little ice pixie holding onto a big bag.

"Hello, I'm Freya," said the pixie. "I've been waiting for you. I knew your magic ice pony would bring you here."

Freya handed Evie an invitation.

"It's for the Ice Queen's birthday party," she said.

"How exciting!" Evie gasped. "But I haven't got a present for her."

"We can give her this," said Freya, and she pulled a beautiful rainbow balloon from her bag.

Just then, an icy gust of wind blew the balloon out of Freya's hands. Sparkles leapt up and caught its ribbons but the wind was so strong that the balloon lifted him up into the air.

"Hold on, Sparkles!" shouted Princess Evie.

Evie and Freya jumped onto Shimmer's back.

Shimmer galloped through the trees,

and jumped across mountain streams,

following Sparkles as he rose higher and higher.

"Miaow!" yelped Sparkles, still clinging
to the balloon's silk ribbons.
"Don't worry," said Evie, "we'll get you down!"

Princess Evie searched through her rucksack of useful things and found a ball, a notebook and a shiny red whistle.

“Oh dear!” sighed Evie. “None of these things can help.”

“I have an idea,” Freya smiled. “Watch!”

Freya began to play a strange tune on the whistle. Instantly, two glittering snowflakes fell from the clouds and, as they fluttered down, they turned into . . .

. . . snowflake fairies!

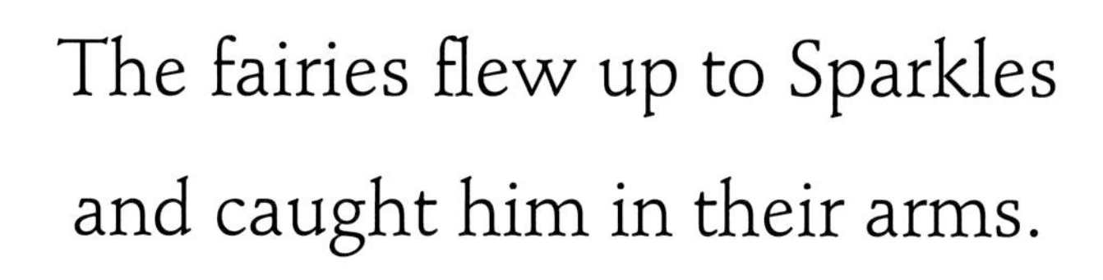

The fairies flew up to Sparkles
and caught him in their arms.

Shimmer neighed, and Evie and Freya cheered
as the snowflake fairies gently floated down,
bringing Sparkles with them.

Sparkles felt a little dizzy but he wasn't hurt. "You're so brave," said Evie. She gave him a big hug.

"Thank you, snowflake fairies."

Suddenly, there was a huge **BANG!** The rainbow balloon caught on a sharp branch and burst.

"Oh dear! What can we give the Queen now?" asked Evie.

“We can make a tiara and necklace,” said Freya. “Look!” The balloon’s silk ribbons were covered in icicles and snowflakes. They glittered like diamonds.

Everyone set to work, making the Queen’s beautiful birthday presents.

Soon the icicle tiara and snowflake necklace shimmered.

It was time for the party!

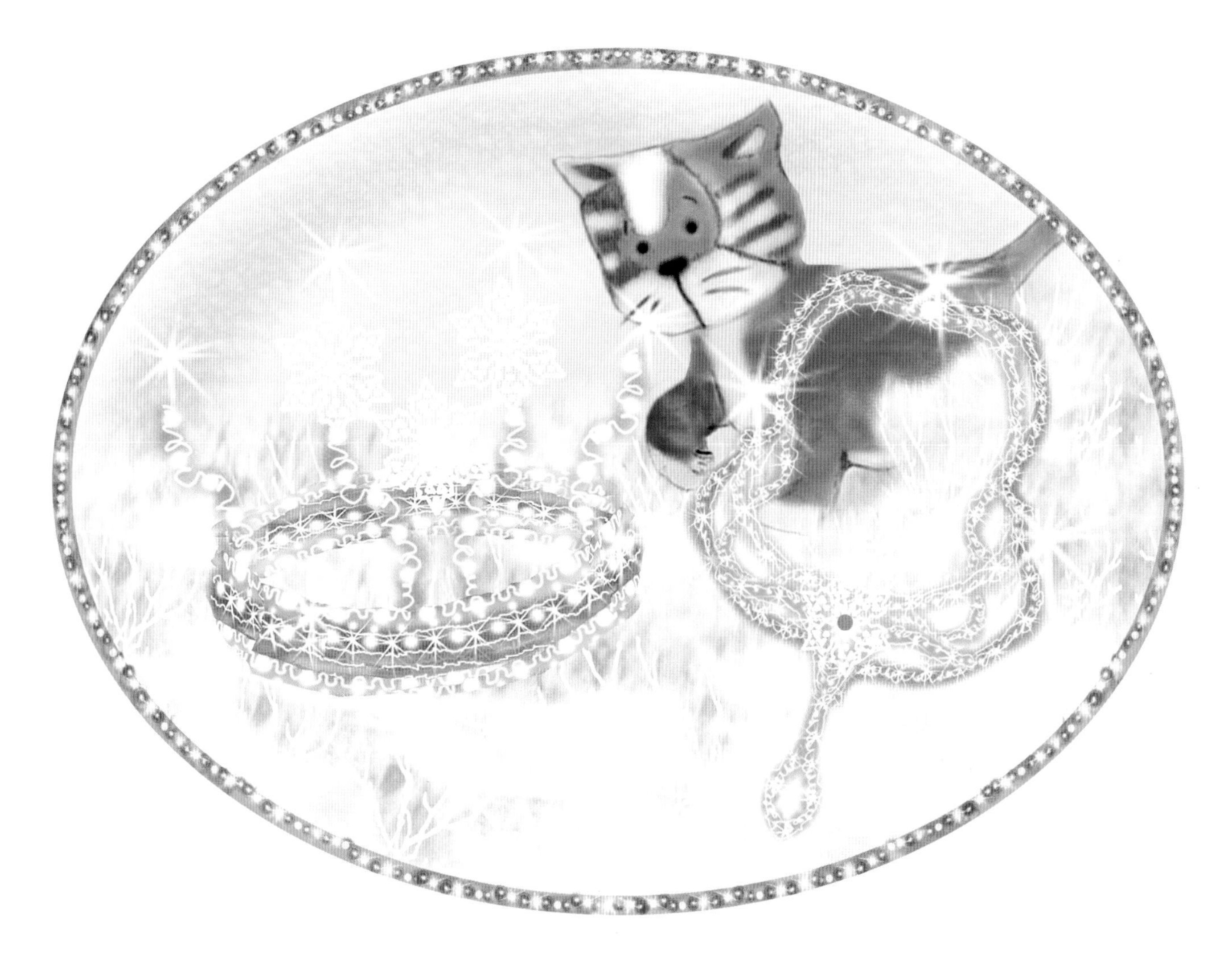

Off Shimmer trotted, taking Evie, Freya and Sparkles to the Ice Palace. The snowflake fairies followed above.

The Ice Palace glittered and sparkled. All the ice pixies were there to celebrate. Even the penguins had come, dressed in their smartest suits to perform their favourite songs.

The Ice Queen looked beautiful in her tiara and matching necklace.
"Would you like to help me blow out my candles?" the Queen asked Evie. "There are so many of them!"

Soon the moon shone in the sky. Princess Evie yawned.
She knew that Shimmer and Sparkles must be tired too.
It was time to go home.

“Thank you so much for inviting us,” she said to the
Ice Queen. “And thank you, Freya.”
“Come again soon!” smiled Freya, as she gave them all a big hug.

Princess Evie waved to her
new friend as she disappeared
through the tunnel of trees.

When they got back to Starlight Stables, large snowflakes began to fall. “It’s snowing!” said Evie. As she put a warm blanket over Shimmer, she noticed a glittery silk ribbon in her mane.

"A snowflake necklace!" said Evie. "Thank you, Freya.
And thank you, Shimmer, for helping Sparkles.
What a very brave ice pony you are!"

"Miaow!" agreed Sparkles.